A Christmas Carol

Book by
CHRISTOPHER BEDLOE

Adaptation and lyrics by
JAMES WOOD

Music by
MALCOLM SHAPCOTT

Based on the Story by Charles Dickens

Samuel French — London
New York — Sydney — Toronto — Hollywood

CHARACTERS

BALLOON LADY
HOT CHESTNUT MAN
POULTERER
EBENEZER SCROOGE
BOB CRATCHIT
FRED
MRS GOODHEART
MISS GOODHEART
GHOST OF JACOB MARLEY
SPIRIT OF CHRISTMAS PAST
SCHOOLMASTER
SCROOGE as a BOY
FAN
MR FEZZIWIG
BELLE
SCROOGE as a YOUNG MAN
MRS FEZZIWIG
DICK WILKINS
FIDDLER
2nd DAUGHTER
MAID
OSTLER
SPIRIT OF CHRISTMAS PRESENT
CROSSING SWEEPER
HOLLY SELLER
TINY TIM
MRS CRATCHIT
PETER
BOY
GIRL
BELINDA
MARTHA
FRED'S WIFE
WIFE'S SISTER
TOPPER
SPIRIT OF CHRISTMAS YET TO COME (non-speaking)
JOE
MRS DILBER
CHARWOMAN

Ladies, Gentlemen, Urchins, Carol Singers, Servants, etc.

Most of the parts can be doubled. The show can be staged quite
satisfactorily with a total cast of 18 - 20 people.

A CHRISTMAS CAROL

STAVE ONE

Scene I

The overture ends with the sound of the city clocks chiming
the hour. The house lights dim as the chimes begin. On the
first stroke of three o'clock the curtain rises, the stage lights
fade up, and are fully up by the last stroke. There is a gauze,
and behind it can be seen a London street, quite immobile. It is
a dark foggy Christmas Eve, and the light comes from a street
lamp, and bright shop windows. R. is the doorway and window
of Scrooge and Marley. One candle glimmers through the window.
L.C. is a poulterers' shop, hanging with dressed birds. The
gauze rises and the scene bursts into a bustle of life. A group
of excited children dance round. As they sing they are watched
benevolently by passers-by.

CHILDREN   SONG: "Half a day to Christmas"

> Now that it's only half a day to Christmas –
> Isn't it grand that Christmas is so near.
> It don't seem right
> To sleep tonight
> Because it's quite the most exciting time of year.
> Isn't it grand it's half a day to Christmas,
> No other day can ever be the same.
> The air is full of magic, if you will believe,
> Half of **a day to Christmas**
> Half of a day to Christmas
> It's Christmas Eve.
>
> Isn't it grand it's half a day to Christmas –
> Everyone is full of Christmas cheer,
> And ev'ry light
> Is twice as bright
> They simply have to shine when Christmas time
>   is here.
> Isn't it grand it's half a day to Christmas,
> Even the streets of London are aglow.

Then all the world is your neighbour, no one
                has to grieve,
Half of a day to Christmas
Half of a day to Christmas
It's Christmas Eve.

Isn't it grand it's half a day to Christmas –
Holly and ivy hanging ev'rywhere.
You want a beau
Then mistletoe
Is there for catching ev'ry bachelor his share.
Isn't it grand it's half a day to Christmas
Isn't it grand with Christmas on the way.
Start a-letting your hair down, ev'ryone is gay,
Half of a day to Christmas
Half of a day to Christmas
Tomorrow will be Christmas Day.

B. LADY   SONG: "Balloons"

Balloons, balloons,
Of ev'ry hue.
Buy one or many
A penny for two.
The games you play
Will carry you away
You'll learn to fly into the sky
Before you wink the other eye.
Balloons, balloons,
For Christmas Day.

HOT C.M.   SONG: "Hot Chestnuts"

Hot chestnuts, hot chestnuts,
Just buy a bag or two.
The whole darn lot
Is piping hot
Specially roasted for you.
Hot chestnuts, hot chestnuts,
A penny's all you pay.
You can't resist that lovely smell
They'll help to warm your hands as well –
Hot chestnuts, hot chestnuts
All fresh today.

POULT.   SONG: "Prime Norfolk Turkey"

Come and buy Norfolk Turkey
You should try Norfolk Turkey

Only my Norfolk Turkeys
Are the best.
See this fine Norfolk Turkey
It's a prime Norfolk Turkey
With a plump and tender breast.
If you want a goose,
They're here to choose,
No gander could be grander than these.
If you fancy duck
Then you're in luck –
They're fresh today from Aylesbury
And guaranteed to please.
Feast your eyes on this Turkey
What a size is this Turkey
It's the prize Norfolk Turkey of the year
All succulent for some rich gent
The prize Norfolk Turkey, what a size Norfolk
Turkey,
The prize Norfolk Turkey is here.

(Children Carol Singers appear, carrying a lantern.
They group round the door of SCROOGE and
MARLEY, and as they begin to sing "God Rest Ye
Merry Gentlemen", SCROOGE enters R., crosses
to his door and lays about him with his stick.)

SCROOGE   God rest ye merry gentlemen indeed! God rest ye
idle beggars, more like. Be off with ye afore I
have the law on ye. Away!

(He goes through his door. The crowd laugh, comfort the carol singers.)

Reprise final half verse: "Half a day to Christmas".

Scene 2

SCROOGE's Office. The scenery has swung round
so that the door to the office is now L., and the
candle is seen to be on BOB CRATCHIT's high desk.
He is copying letters industriously as SCROOGE
removes his hat, coat and scarf.

SCROOGE   Not finished yet, Cratchit? You must apply yourself more diligently to your task.

BOB   It's my hands, Mr. Scrooge, sir, they're so cold.
(He comes forward diffidently with a small coal
shovel.) Do you think, sir, I could have another
piece of coal?

SCROOGE   Another piece, sirrah? You've already had one
            today! If this feckless extravagance continues, I
            can see that it will be necessary for us to part!
            Back to your work!

            (BOB retires quickly to his seat, and as he tries
            to warm his hands round his candle there is a loud
            knocking on the door.)

            (Moving D.R.)   See who that is, Cratchit.

BOB   (with alacrity)   Yes, Mr. Scrooge, sir.

            (He goes to the door, but FRED bursts in.)

FRED   Oho.

BOB   Oh, Mr. Frea.

FRED   Yes, and a merry Christmas to you, Bob Cratchit.

BOB   (going over to SCROOGE)   It's Mr. Fred, your
            nephew, sir.

SCROOGE   (as if to himself)   Bah. Come to wish me a merr;
            Christmas, I'll be bound.

FRED   And a merry Christmas to you, uncle. God save
            you.

SCROOGE   I knew it.   (To FRED.)   Bah. Humbug.

FRED   Christmas a humbug, uncle? You don't mean that,
            I'm sure?

SCROOGE   I do mean it. Merry Christmas – what right have
            you to be merry? What reason have you to be
            merry, you're poor enough.

FRED   Come, then. What reason have you to be dismal?
            You're rich enough.

SCROOGE   Bah.

            SONG: "Christmas is Humbug"

                Christmas is humbug
                It's sentimental rot
                There's nothing good about it to be said.
                With people spending money that they simply
                                        haven't got
                While their bank account slips further in the red.
                This merry Christmas nonsense never did 'em
                                        any good,

But a fool and his money soon will part.
Let each merry Christmas idiot be boiled with
                                    his pud
And a stake of holly hammered through his heart.
Christmas - is humbug.

FRED   (spoken)   Oh come, uncle!

              (sung)

              Christmas is Christmas
              A season of goodwill
              A time to be forgiving, to be kind.
              The Christmas message may not put a penny in
                                        the till
              But it brings a true contentment to the mind.
              It's the one time in the calendar when man can
                                        speak to man
              Instead of as a master to a slave
              It brings the understanding that only Christmas
                                        can -
              The lesson's there to learn it if we only can
                                        discern it
              As we make our common journey to the grave.
              Christmas - God bless it.

BOB   (spoken)   Amen, amen.   (He applauds.)

SCROOGE   (spoken)   Let me hear another sound from you,
              and you'll celebrate Christmas by losing your
              situation.   (To FRED.)   You're a powerful
              speaker, sir, I wonder you don't go into Parlia-
              ment.   (He sings.)

              On the day that my partner Jacob Marley died
              I felt that the occasion needed marking,
              So his memory was suitably sanctified
              By sealing a most profitable bargain.
              He died seven years ago today
              And I know that he'd support me when I say -

              Christmas is humbug
              It's nothing but a trick
              That's fostered by the hypocrites and such
              When paupers and beggars and folk who live on
                                        tick
              Come wheedling and whining for a touch.
              Take Cratchit here, my clerk, earning half-a-
                                        crown a day

> With a wife and seven children to support,
> Pretending to be merry, on his holiday with pay
> It's my pocket that he's picking
> When my boots he should be licking, how I wish
>   I could dismiss him for his sport.
> Christmas – is humbug.

FRED   Well, in spite of all that, uncle, come, dine with us on Christmas Day tomorrow. My wife will be glad to welcome you.

SCROOGE   I'll see you both in hell first. Good afternoon.

FRED   Why – why?

SCROOGE   Why did you get married?

FRED   Because I fell in love.

SCROOGE   In love? Bah!

FRED   Why can't we be friends, uncle? I want nothing of you. I have no quarrel with you.

SCROOGE   Good afternoon.

FRED   Well, I made the effort in homage to Christmas, so I'll keep my Christmas humour to the last. A merry Christmas, uncle.

SCROOGE   Good afternoon.

FRED   A merry Christmas to you, Bob.

SCROOGE   Good afternoon.

FRED   And a happy New Year.

BOB   And the same to you, Mr. Fred.

          (FRED goes to the door. At the same time, two ladies enter. FRED bows them in and then goes.)

MRS. G.   Scrooge and Marley's, I believe?

BOB   (hurrying forward)   Indeed it is, madam. Do come –

SCROOGE   Get back to your work, sirrah.

          (BOB goes quickly back to his desk, and writes industriously throughout the next scene.)

MRS. G.   Have I the pleasure of addressing Mr. Scrooge or Mr. Marley?

SCROOGE   Mr. Marley has been dead these seven years, madam. He died this very night seven years ago.

MRS. G.	Oh, that is sad, is it not, daughter, and on Christmas Eve too?
MISS G.	It is sad indeed, ma'am.
MRS. G.	But we have no doubt that his generosity is well represented by his surviving partner.
SCROOGE	His generosity - ?
MRS. G.	At this festive season of the year, Mr. Scrooge, a few of us are endeavouring to raise a fund to buy some meat and drink, and a means of warmth for the poor and destitute. They suffer greatly, and even more so at the present time.
MISS G.	Many thousands are in want of common necessaries.
MRS. G.	Hundreds of thousands are in want of common comforts, sir.
SCROOGE	(sings) Are there no prisons?
MRS. G.	Plenty of prisons. SING
SCROOGE	Are there no workhouses?
MISS G.	Oh, yes indeed. SING
SCROOGE	Have the Tread Mill and the Poor Law ceased to function?
MRS. G.	Unhappily, no, sir. SING
SCROOGE	I subscribe to these without the least compunction. By what logic should I have to pay again?
MISS G.	But many won't be seen in such a place. SING
MRS. G.	They'd rather die than suffer the disgrace. SING.
SCROOGE	(spoken) Rather die, would they? Then they had better do it.

(Sings.)

        Charity is humbug
        At any time of year.
        The idle always suffer from starvation
        If they want to die of hunger who am I to interfere?
        It will help decrease the surplus population.
        And just because it's Christmas you expect me to
                                        donate
        To keep them in their idleness and sloth.

Your continued presence here, ma'am, will
merely aggravate
So I'll say Good afternoon and now be off.

MRS. G.	But Mr. Scrooge –
SCROOGE	Good afternoon.
MISS G.	Where's your compassion?
SCROOGE	I said be off.
MRS. G.	Your milk of human kindness –
SCROOGE	Get off my premises. (He pushes them out.) Humbug!

(The city clock chimes seven.   CRATCHIT closes
his ledger with a bang.)

You'll want all day tomorrow, I suppose?

BOB   If quite convenient, sir.

SCROOGE   It's not convenient, and it's not fair. If I was to
stop half a crown for it, you'd think yourself ill-
used, I'll be bound. And yet you don't think me
ill-used, when I pay a day's wages for no work.
(He starts to put on his outdoor clothes.)

BOB   But it's only once a year, sir.

SCROOGE   A poor excuse for picking a man's pocket every
twenty-fifth of December. But I suppose you must
have the whole day. Be here all the earlier next
morning.

BOB   Oh, I will, sir, I will.

SCROOGE goes out. To the music of "Christmas
Eve", BOB clears up his papers, chuckling aloud,
wraps his long comforter around his neck, blows
out his candle, and goes out with the stage almost
in darkness except for the light from the poulterers'
shop which still shines through the window.

The gauze comes down again, and SCROOGE's
front door is wheeled on D.C. MARLEY is concealed behind it. The only light is a spot on the
door.

Scene 3

Enter SCROOGE L. He is muttering to himself.

SCROOGE   Merry Christmas, indeed. If any other man wishes
          me a merry Christmas, I'll wring his neck. All I
          ask is to be left to myself. I'll make me a nice
          bowl of gruel, and spend the evening totting up my
          cash book. The best Christmas present is a
          balanced book of accounts.

          (SCROOGE fumbles for his key. He is about to
          put it in the lock when the knocker dissolves to
          reveal the face of JACOB MARLEY. Sound
          effect of whining wind. SCROOGE drops back,
          aghast.)

          Marley! Jacob Marley's face!

          (The effect fades, and the door is restored to
          normal.)

          He's gone. Why, he was never there at all. Just
          a trick of the senses. A slight disorder of the
          stomach makes them cheats.

          SONG: "Indigestion"

               You were not an apparition
               But a medical condition.
               This extraordinary suggestion
               Was a touch of - indigestion.

               A bit of underdone potato,
               Half-digested slice of veal,
               Blot of mustard, spot of sago,
               Or a bit of jellied eel.
               A crumb of cheese most likely was the knave.
               There's more in you of gravy than the grave.

               P'raps those oysters that I fancied
               Were just slightly on the turn,
               Or the butter going rancid -
               Too long parted from the churn.
               A touch of colic likely is the knave.
               .There's more in you of gravy than the grave.

               A spoonful of bicarbonate
               Will very soon alleviate
               The ill that made my senses misbehave -
               There's more in you of gravy
               Than the grave.

          Fully restored in confidence he unlocks the door
          and opens it as the gauze rises. He goes through

the door, which then disappears.

Scene 4

SCROOGE's room. The fireplace is D.L., the
window above it. A fourposter bed R.C., with the
head just in the wings. Upstage behind the bed is
a black drape. As SCROOGE enters the room it is
in darkness. He lights a candle, and the lights
fade up slightly as he carries the candle round
looking in corners and under the bed to make sure
MARLEY is not there, muttering the while, "Marley
- humbug."   Feeling secure again, he takes off
hat and coat, puts on his nightcap and prepares
his gruel over the fire. While doing all this he
sings.

SCROOGE   SONG: "Fine Man of Business"

Jacob Marley was a fine man of business
He taught me nearly everything I know
Of how to scrape and screw
That extra bob or two
From people with an intellect financially slow.
Oh, the markets that he cornered and monopolised,
The percentages he managed to obtain.
He was quite the finest partner that a man could
                              hope to have
Jacob Marley had a very cunning brain.

Jacob Marley was a fine man of business
He knew the price of every stock and share
And while adding huge amounts
To his capital accounts
He got a lot of pleasure driving others to despair.
Oh, the bankruptcies, the failures, the suicides,
At times we had one nearly every week.
When it came to making profits all his rivals
                              would admit
Jacob Marley had a very fine technique.

Jacob Marley was a fine man of business,
With his balance sheet imprinted on his soul.
He had a sort of feel
For a profitable deal
And never once let sentiment divert him from his
                              goal.
He'd manipulate the market quite outrageously,

And never missed a chance from first to last.
When it came to striking bargains at the other
                              chap's expense
Jacob Marley was completely unsurpassed.

Yes, a fine, fine man of business.

(As the song ends, lights dim, wind effect again,
clanking chains. SCROOGE cowers in his chair
with basin of gruel on his lap. His wooden spoon
is rattling against the basin. MARLEY appears in
front of the black drape, lit in green. He comes
slowly D.S.)

SCROOGE	How now, what do you want with me?
MARLEY	Much.
SCROOGE	Who are you?
MARLEY	Ask me rather who I was.
SCROOGE	Who were you, then?
MARLEY	In life I was your partner, Jacob Marley.
SCROOGE	(rising) Can you – can you sit down?
MARLEY	I can.
SCROOGE	Do it, then.

(MARLEY sits in SCROOGE's chair. SCROOGE
backs away.)

MARLEY	So you don't believe in me.
SCRÓOGE	I don't.
MARLEY	You doubt your senses.
SCROOGE	I do. You're a humbug, I tell you, humbug.

(MARLEY gives a fearful cry, rises, clanks his
chains and turns green again.)

SCROOGE	Mercy, mercy. (On his knees.) Dreadful apparition, why do you trouble me?
MARLEY	Man of the worldly mind, do you believe in me or not?
SCROOGE	I do, I must. But why do spirits walk the earth, and why do they come to me?
MARLEY	SONG: "I Wear The Chain I Forged in Life"

It is required of every man that his spirit
should go forth
And travel far and wide among his fellows.
If it does not so in life, it must do so after death
In limbo, with the spectres and the shadows.
These seven years trapped, and tortured by
remorse,
Observe me, Ebenezer, lest you tread the self
same course.

(He gives a fearful cry again. SCROOGE cowers.)

SCROOGE (spoken)   You are fettered – tell me why.

MARLEY   I wear the chain I forged in life
I made it link by link
Ignoring want and misery
Of fellow men surrounding me
I never paused to think
Beyond our money-changing hole
Where avarice devoured the soul
And left me with the torment and the pain
Of the chain I forged in life.

(He gives another dismal cry.)

SCROOGE (spoken)   Oh, please don't do that, Jacob. Speak
comfort to me, Jacob.

MARLEY   (spoken)   Comfort? I have none to give. (Sings.)

The chain you bear was much as mine
Full seven years ago.
Since then with screw and scrape and pinch
You've added to it inch by inch
And I have watched it grow.
Till now its length is wondrous
Its weight is great and ponderous
And when you die the prize you will obtain
Is the chain you forged in life.

(He clanks his chain.)

SCROOGE Oh, don't be hard on me, Jacob. You were always
a good man of business.

MARLEY   Business, business. Mankind should have been my
business; the common welfare should have been my
business; charity, mercy, forbearance and bene-
volence should all have been my business.

SCROOGE Is there no escape, Jacob? Is there no hope for me?

MARLEY	I am here tonight to warn you, and to tell you that you have yet a chance and hope of escaping my fate. A chance and hope of _my_ procuring, Ebenezer.
SCROOGE	Thankee, Jacob. You were always a good friend to me.
MARLEY	You will be haunted by three spirits.
SCROOGE	Is that the chance and hope you mentioned, Jacob?
MARLEY	It is.
SCROOGE	I - I think I'd rather not.
MARLEY	Without their visits you cannot hope to shun the path I tread. Expect the first tomorrow when the bell tolls one.
SCROOGE	Couldn't I take them all at once, and have it over, Jacob?
MARLEY	Expect the second on the next night at the same hour. And the third upon the next night when the last stroke of twelve has ceased to vibrate. (He begins to disappear.) Look to see me no more. But look that, for your own sake, you remember what has passed between us. (He disappears.)
	(SCROOGE waits for a moment, then with a shuddering cry leaps into bed and draws the curtains. His candle gutters out, a clock chimes and strikes one. SCROOGE's curtains fly back, and in a pool of brilliant light there stands the SPIRIT OF CHRISTMAS PAST.)
SCROOGE	(with sheet up to his chin) Are you the spirit, sir, whose coming was foretold to me?
PAST	I am.
SCROOGE	Who and what are you?
PAST	I am the Ghost of Christmas Past.
SCROOGE	Long past?
PAST	No. Your past.
SCROOGE	I wonder if you would oblige me, sir, by putting on your cap.
PAST	What! Would you so soon put out the light that

shines from me? The light that may lead you to
your one hope of salvation?

SCROOGE   I beg your pardon, sir. I had no wish to offend.
May I ask your business with me?

PAST   Your welfare.

SCROOGE   I am greatly obliged to you, sir, though I cannot
help but think that a good night's sleep would be
more to my benefit.

PAST   Your reclamation, then. Take heed. Rise, and
walk with me.

The GHOST helps SCROOGE from his bed and
they come D.S. together. The tabs close. Sound
and lighting effects.

Scene 5

This scene is played to white tabs, with lighting
effects.

SCROOGE   (breathless)   Not so fast, good spirit, I am only
mortal.

PAST   Bear but a touch of my hand. Our journey is
almost over.

(Sound fades to silence.)

Do you recognise this place?

SCROOGE   Good Heaven! I was bred in this place. I was a
boy here. This is the road I walked along. I know
every gate and every tree. And here is the sign-
post to the little town. Look, there in the valley,
the river, the bridge and the church.

PAST   And the school.

SCROOGE   (sadly)   Ah, the school.

PAST   It is Christmas Eve, but the school is not quite
deserted. A solitary child is left there still,
neglected by his friends.

SCROOGE   (almost sobbing)   I know it – I know it.

PAST   Look here.

The tabs part.

Scene 6

A schoolroom. A boy sits reading on a high stool.
He is lit by a spot. As SCROOGE watches, the
boy lowers his book and begins to sob.

SCROOGE   Poor boy, poor boy! I was lonely, d'you see? I
            wish - I wish - but it's too late now.

PAST   What's the matter?

SCROOGE   Nothing, nothing. There were boys singing a
            Christmas carol at my door yesterday. I would
            like to have given them something, that's all. But
            it's too late now. Five years I was at that school,
            and never a happy moment.

PAST   But do you remember the day you left?

MASTER   (off)   Master Scrooge. Master Scrooge.

            (Enter SCHOOLMASTER. He is a terrifying
            figure in tattered gown. The boy leaps up and
            cowers against the wall.)

            (Oily.)   Ah, Master Scrooge.

BOY   Sir?

MASTER   Still at your books, I see. Your avidity in the
            pursuit of knowledge is most gratifying, sir.

BOY   Sir?

MASTER   We have a visitor for you, Master Scrooge. Your
            sister has come to see you.

BOY   My sister?

MASTER   Come in, young lady, come in.

            (Enter FAN.)

            Here is the young gentleman, educated and ready
            for the world. Language is not powerful enough to
            describe this infant phenomenon.

            (FAN and the BOY embrace.)

BOY   Fan, my little sister! Let me look at you. You are
            grown into quite a little woman.

FAN   And you a man, dear brother. I have come to bring
            you home.

BOY   Home, little Fan?

MASTER	Yes, Home, Master Scrooge. (He goes to shake hands with the boy, who ducks involuntarily.) And since you are now to leave my educational establishment, you must take wine with me. (He produces a decanter and three glasses, pours the wine, downs his own, saying "Your good health", and retrieves the other two glasses almost untouched. During the next song, he drinks these two and helps himself liberally so that at the end he is joining in with abandon.)
BOY	Is it really true, Fan?
FAN	Yes, Ebenezer, you are coming home for good and all. Home for ever and ever.

TRIO: "Going Home"

FAN	Going home, going home, Going home to stay.
BOY	Schooldays are over now What a wonderful day.
FAN	Going home, going home, Quickly as we can. Today you may be still a boy Tomorrow you'll be a man. Don't delay, pack your case, Bring your coat, Let's away from the place Hurry 'cos the coach is waiting.
BOTH	Going home, going home
FAN	To Father dear and me He's so much kinder now Than he used ever to be. That was why I told him I Was miserable on my own And life would not be happy again Till I knew you were coming home.
BOY	Going home, going home To Father dear and you This day I've dreamed about Can't believe that it's true.
BOTH	Going home, going home, Leaving for good and all
BOY	And soon the school will only be A memory to recall.
FAN	Oh what fun life will be

	When you're home
	You're the one dear to me
	We will have such times together.
BOTH	Going home, going home,
	Never returning here
	Life now is sweeter than
	It's been for many a year.
BOY	Going home, going home,
	Together for Christmas Day
FAN	And this will be the merriest ever
	For having you home to stay.

MASTER   So farewell, Ebenezer,
We're sorry you must go
Your departure is particularly sad for me,
For the loss of your fees are
A sad financial blow
To the pocket of the head of this Academy.
Going home, going home,
Ready to face the world.
Proud with the flag of knowledge
Constantly unfurled.
Going home, going home,
Classically complete.
A Latin verb will always help you
Stand on your own two feet.

BOY   Now it's time to be gone,
Sir, goodbye.
Thank you for all you've done.

MASTER   Ebenezer, it was nothing.

ALL   Going home, going home,
Never returning here.
Life now is sweeter than
It's been for many a year.

BOY & FAN   Going home, going home,
Going home to stay
And we'll be spending Christmas together
So this will be the merriest ever.

MASTER   Yes, this will be the merriest ever.

BOY & FAN   Together for Christmas Day.

    Tabs close.

Scene 7

    Played in front of tabs.

PAST   She was always a delicate creature, whom a breath

might have withered, but she had a generous heart.

SCROOGE   So she had, you're right. I will not deny it,
           Spirit. God forbid.

PAST   She died a woman, and had, as I think, children.

SCROOGE   One child.

PAST   True. Your nephew, Fred.

SCROOGE   (uneasy)   Yes.

PAST   Ah, here we are. We have arrived at our next
           destination.

           The tabs part.

Scene 8

           FEZZIWIG's Office. There is a door U.C. with
           a step leading to it. This is the entrance to the
           office from the rest of the house. FEZZIWIG's
           desk is on a small dais U.R. There are two desks
           for young SCROOGE and DICK WILKINS left. As
           the lights fade up these desks are unoccupied.
           FEZZIWIG and his daughter BELLE are frozen
           D.C.

PAST   Do you know it?

SCROOGE   (circling the office and characters) Know it? I
           was apprenticed here. And there's old Fezziwig,
           bless his heart. It's Fezziwig alive again. And
           Belle - sweet little Belle. Ah, dear.

PAST   You seem regretful.

SCROOGE   It's just that - things might have been different if -
           but never mind.

           (FEZZIWIG and BELLE come to life. She is tying
           her bonnet and putting on her muff.)

FEZZIWIG   My dear, you must wrap up warmly if you are to go
           out on such a night. Must you really go?

BELLE   I must, father. Dick Wilkins' poor mother is so
           very ill, and I think she looks forward to my visits.

FEZZIWIG   I'm sure she does, my dear, I'm sure she does.
           But I sometimes wish you would think less of com-
           forting others and a little more of yourself.

BELLE   Of myself, father?

FEZZIWIG   Yes. It's time, you know, that you were thinking
             of finding a nice young man to be a husband to you.

BELLE   Oh, father.

FEZZIWIG   Well, here you are, as pretty as a picture. There
             must be lots of young fellows only too eager to call
             upon you, if only you would give them a little en-
             couragement.

BELLE   (laughing)   I expect there are. But any young
             man won't do for me.   (Sings.)

             SONG: "Heart of Gold"

                  I don't intend to be swept off my feet
                  By the first young man who comes to woo me.
                  For I know in the end I am sure to meet
                  The one who will love me truly.
                  And my sort of man
                  Is a shy sort of man,
                  So I'll wait till I find the right sort of man for
                                                              me.

                  I look for a man with a heart of gold
                  To cherish and love me
                  Be tender and kind
                  Put no one above me
                  That's the man that I plan to find.
                  I look for a man with a heart of gold,
                  And once I have found him
                  I know we will share
                  A love quite unbounded
                  A devotion beyond compare.
                  And we'll soon discover happiness we've never
                                                         known,
                  With a heart of gold I can hold for my very own.

FEZZIWIG   My dear, these are fine and noble thoughts, but a
             true and unselfish love is a very rare thing. You
             may be searching for an ideal that does not exist.

BELLE   Do not worry, father, I shall find him one day,
             never fear.

             (She kisses her father and goes out quickly R. He
             is left shaking his head. The lights fade on the set;
             spot up on SCROOGE and SPIRIT.)

SCROOGE	Spirit, show me no more. Conduct me home, I beg you.
PAST	One shadow more. The time has past, and three years have gone by. And now it is Christmas Eve.
SCROOGE	I remember it.

(Spot fades, set lights up. FEZZIWIG is at his desk U.R., EBENEZER and DICK WILKINS are at their desks L. They are writing industriously. As the lights fade up, a clock strikes seven. They all look up eagerly and put their work aside. FEZZIWIG jumps to his feet, rubs his hands together and bursts out laughing.)

FEZZIWIG	Yo ho, my boys, no more work tonight. Christmas Eve, Dick. Christmas Eve, Ebenezer. Let's have the shutters up before a man can say Jack Robinson.

(They push the desks aside, sweep the floor. All is bustle and excitement.)

Clear away, my lads, and let's have lots of room here. Hilli-ho, Dick. Chirrup, Ebenezer.

(A burst of laughter is heard outside.)

Hurry, lads, hurry, I can hear them all coming. Let's have it snug and warm and bright as a ball-room.

EBENEZER	We're nearly ready, sir.

(Enter MRS. FEZZIWIG carrying a bowl of punch; BELLE and second daughter carrying glasses. A kitchen maid and an ostler.)

FEZZIWIG	We're ready for you, my dear, we're ready. You have come at just the right moment as always. And bearing the festive spirit, too.
MRS. F.	A merry Christmas to you, one and all. Now let us all join in drinking a glass of my own special punch.

(There is a chorus of "Merry Christmas", and the two daughters ladle out the punch and hand it round amid general cheers and laughter. DICK WILKINS jumps up on to the little dais on which stands MR. FEZZIWIG's desk.)

DICK	A toast, a toast. Let us drink to Mr. Fezziwig, the best employer a man could have. And to Mrs.

Fezziwig.

(They all drink with acclamations.)

FEZZIWIG   Thankee, Dick, thankee. Thanks to all of you.
But come, 'tis time the dancing began. What has
happened to the fiddler?

(Enter FIDDLER, insinuating himself through the
crowd.)

FIDDLER   Here-I am, Mr. Fezziwig.

FEZZIWIG   So there you are; why, man, you look an uncommon
doleful fiddler for such a gay occasion. We must
liven you up with a glass of punch.

(BELLE brings one.)

Now, down in one, man. Down in one.

ALL   Down in one. That's the way.

(The FIDDLER drinks it down at a gulp. All cheer.
He becomes skittish, jumps on the dais, and begins
tuning up. All clap.)

FEZZIWIG   That's more like it. Now to it, lads. Mrs. Fezziwig
and I will lead the dance. I vow the seasonal spirit
is in my feet already.

MRS. F.   Lor', Mr. Fezziwig, to be sure, to be sure.

SONG: "Fezziwig's Ball"

(The song is arranged so that each couple who
come to the front in the dance have a verse.)

FEZZIWIG   Folk who live in the house of Fezziwig
& MRS. F.   Workers, family, one and all,
              Christmas Eve in the house of Fezziwig,
              Come to Fezziwig's Ball.

BELLE &   Those who work for the house of Fezziwig,
EBENEZER   Old ones, young ones, great and small,
              Christmas Eve in the house of Fezziwig
              Come to Fezziwig's Ball.

ALL   Give three cheers for Fezziwig
              Here's to Fezziwig
              Bless his heart.
              God bless Mrs. Fezziwig,
              And the Fezziwigs' party.

(16 bars dance.)

MISS F. & DICK	Grab your partners here at Fezziwig, Up the middle and down the hall. Christmas Eve in the house of Fezziwig Come to Fezziwig's Ball.

MAID & OSTLER   No more work today at Fezziwig,
Nothing but fun for one and all,
Christmas Eve in the house of Fezziwig
Come to Fezziwig's Ball.

ALL   Give three cheers for Fezziwig,
Here's to Fezziwig
Bless his heart.
God bless Mrs. Fezziwig,
And the Fezziwigs' party.

No one sleeps in the house of Fezziwig,
Everyone dance to the fiddler's call.
Christmas Eve in the house of Fezziwig,
Come to Fezziwig's Ball.

Give three cheers for Fezziwig,
Here's to Fezziwig
Bless his heart.
God bless Mrs. Fezziwig,
God bless Mr. Fezziwig,
Bless the Fezziwigs all.
Give three cheers for one and all,
Fezziwigs' Ball.

FEZZIWIG   (out of breath)   Enough, enough. I cannot dance
another step until I have eaten. Come everybody,
into the parlour. There's cold roast.

MRS. F.   And cold boiled.

BELLE   And cake.

MISS F.   And mince pies.

FEZZIWIG   And plenty of beer. Come, let us partake of this
feast.

(They go out noisily C., but EBENEZER detains
BELLE. The lights dim on the set; a spot lights
SCROOGE and the SPIRIT.)

SCROOGE   (excited)   That's just as it was, just as it was.
Oh, I remember it all so clearly. What wonderful
fun we had, and every year the same. What a good

man he was, dear old Fezziwig.

PAST	Come. Such a small matter to make these silly folks so full of gratitude.
SCROOGE	Small?
PAST	Why, is it not? He has spent but a few pounds of his mortal money. Three or four, perhaps. Is that so much?
SCROOGE	It isn't that, it isn't that, Spirit. He had the power to make us happy or unhappy; to make our service light or burdensome, a pleasure or a toil. Why, then, the happiness he gave was as great as if it cost a fortune. (He stops short.)
PAST	What is the matter?
SCROOGE	Nothing particular.
PAST	Something, I think?
SCROOGE	No, no. I was just thinking that I would like to be able to say a word or two to my clerk, Bob Cratchit, that's all.
PAST	(taking his arm) Observe. See what is happening.

(Lights fade up on the set. Spot fades.)

EBENEZER	Belle, why is it that you avoid me so? I can never see you alone.
BELLE	Do you still want to see me, Ebenezer?
EBENEZER	But of course I do. Have we not an understanding that we will be betrothed?
BELLE	Our contract is an old one. Since it was made you have changed. I have watched while all the good in you has been swamped by your passion for gain. Another idol has displaced me. I hope it can comfort you in time to come as I would have done.
EBENEZER	What idol has displaced you?
BELLE	A golden one. (Sings.)

Reprise. "Heart of Gold"

> I looked for a man with a heart of gold
> To cherish and love me,
> Be tender and kind,
> Put no one above me

That's the man that I planned to find.
I looked for a man with a heart of gold.
I thought I had found him
When you came my way
But hope was confounded
All too soon disillusion came,
And I soon discovered what I should have
                                    always known,
That a heart of gold can be cold as a heart of
                                    stone.

EBENEZER (over music)   But, Belle, do you not see? If I
can be rich life will be better for both of us.

BELLE   (over music)   Do not deceive yourself, Ebenezer.
Your greed does not stem from any thought of me.
It is for your own aggrandizement. The man I
marry must love me for myself alone.   (Sings.)

That's the man that I planned to find.
I looked for a man with a heart of gold.
I thought I had found him
When you came my way
But hope was confounded
All too soon disillusion came.
And I soon discovered what I should have
                                    always known,
That a heart of gold can be cold as a heart of
                                    stone.

EBENEZER I have grown this much wiser in the ways of the
world, that I have learned that to be well regarded
you must be wealthy.   (Sings.)

SONG: "Gold"

I cannot understand why our society
Rejects a man who happens to be poor.
Yet equally deplores the impropriety
Of the poor man who attempts to make some more.
I've decided that the only test of rank
Is the credit balance standing in the bank.

Gold, gold, gold,
My need for it is avid,
I've simply got to have it
To be socially elect.
Gold, gold, gold,
At ev'ry chance I grab it,

It's more than just a habit
It's the best thing to collect.
Oh, there's nothing like the jingle of a sovereign
                                        or two,
The sound of it is music to my ears.
And remember all my worldly goods I vow to
                                  share with you,
To keep us in contentment in advancing years.
Gold, gold, gold,
My ambition, my desire
Is to see it mounting higher
Fill the coffers with as much as they will hold,
Of gold, gold, gold.

(During the last lines, FEZZIWIG and all the party have entered and listened.)

BELLE   Oh, Ebenezer, you're hopeless. You just haven't understood a word I have been saying.   (She flounces D.R.)

FEZZIWIG   My boy –   (Sings.)

I'm filled with admiration for your sentiments,
For prudence is a virtue oft neglected.
A rainy day is everyone's presentiment
And always comes when it is least expected.
So save the very most you can afford,
And thrift will surely bring its own reward.

(During the next verse EBENEZER tries to go to BELLE, but is prevented by the rest.)

ALL,   Gold, gold, gold,
EXCEPT   There is no doubt about it
BELLE &   You just can't live without it
EBENEZER   It's the very breath of life.
                      Gold, gold, gold,
                      The man who hasn't got it
                      Is sadly out of pocket
                      When he comes to take a wife.
                      Oh, there's nothing like the jingle of a sovereign
                                                        or two,
                      The sound of it is music to my ears.
                      And once you've got enough of it your dreams
                                                  will all come true,
                      And ev'ry other sort of trouble disappears.
                      Gold, gold, gold,
                      You will never be successful

Till you've got a brimming chestful
Ev'ry single thing of value is controlled
By gold, gold, gold.

(They take the verse again softly. EBENEZER
joins in, carried away by their enthusiasm.
BELLE stands with her back to them, and sings
"Heart of Gold" contra as indicated before making
a tearful exit C., seen only by SCROOGE and the
SPIRIT.)

ALL   BELLE

Gold, gold, gold,
There is no doubt about
                    it
You just can't live
               without it
It's the very
Breath of life   I looked
Gold, gold, gold,
The man who hasn't got   For a man
                    it
Is sadly out of pocket   With a heart of gold,
When he comes to take   To cherish and love me
               a wife.
Oh, there's nothing   Be tender and kind
   like the jingle of a
   sovereign or two
The sound of it is music   Put no one above me
               to my ears.
Ev'ry other sort of   That's the man that I
   trouble disappears.   planned to find.
                              But I soon discovered
                              What I should have
                              Always known –

                              (She goes out.)

Gold, gold, gold.
Oh, you'll never be
   successful
Till you've got a
   brimming chestful
Of that gold –
Of gold, gold, gold,
   gold, gold!

CURTAIN

STAVE TWO

Scene 9

SCROOGE's Bedroom again. As the curtain rises a spot fades up on the bed D.R. The bed curtains are drawn. The rest of the stage is in darkness, but the fireplace is set L.

We can hear snores from the bed. Suddenly there is a prodigious snore and the bed curtains wave. SCROOGE's head appears from between the curtains, and he peers apprehensively round. After a moment a look of relief crosses his face.

SCROOGE   My own room! And my own bed! All is restored to normal! And he's gone, that Ghost of Christmas Past. What a very harrowing experience - and it all happened just as Jacob Marley foretold.   (He pulls aside the curtains and sits on the edge of the bed.)   Now what was it he said? There are still to be two more Spirits. "Expect the second on the next night at the same hour."   (He walks to the foot of the bed as he talks.)   I wonder how long I have been sleeping. What o'clock can it be?

(A clock commences chiming.)

Ah. Providential.   (He listens intently. The clock strikes one.)   One!   (He dives for his bed, and peeps through the curtains. It is evident from their shaking that he is trembling violently.) I must have slept the clock round. Now what frightful visitation am I to expect? Get a grip on yourself, Ebenezer Scrooge. Prepare yourself for the worst.

(There is a silence. SCROOGE begins to look bewildered, then a voice is heard humming, then singing "Good King Wenceslas". The voice gets louder until the last line is bellowed. As the

volume increases so the spot fades up on the
SPIRIT OF CHRISTMAS PRESENT seated by the
fire, which also comes alight. As he sings he is
eating a leg of chicken which he throws over his
shoulder as the song ends. He is a large jolly
fellow, somewhat akin to Santa Claus, in a loose
green garment. He is surrounded by the good
things of Christmas, and SCROOGE's fireplace
is gaily decorated with holly.)

PRESENT   (hums then sings)   Brightly shone the moon that
                                                   night
                                  Tho' the frost was cruel,
                                  When a poor man came in
                                                   sight,
                                  Gathering winter fuel.
(He laughs uproariously.)   Ebenezer Scrooge,
come forth.   Come forth and know me better, man.

(SCROOGE emerges and advances timidly.   He
gazes in wonder.)

Look upon me. I am the Ghost of Christmas
Present. You have never seen the like of me
before?

SCROOGE   Never.

PRESENT   Have you never walked forth with the other
members of my family: meaning my elder brothers
born these latter years?

SCROOGE   I don't think I have. I'm afraid I have not. Have
you had many brothers, Spirit?

PRESENT   Many brothers? More than eighteen hundred. One
for every year of our Lord.

SCROOGE   A tremendous family to provide for.

(The SPIRIT roars with laughter.)

Spirit, conduct me where you will. I went forth
last night on compulsion, and I learnt a lesson
which is working now. Tonight, if you have aught
to teach me, let me profit by it.

PRESENT   I am glad to hear that you are in a mood to profit
by what I shall show you, for today is Christmas
Day, when the Spirit of Christmas is truly abroad.
We shall see how the people celebrate this great

occasion. First I will show you the streets of London.

SCROOGE   But I know the streets of London.

PRESENT   I doubt if you do. They are very different today. Come. Touch my robe.

(The lights dim out quickly. Sound effect of rushing wind. White tabs close and gauze as Scene 3.)

Scene 10

(SCROOGE and SPIRIT enter R. and cross L.)

SCROOGE   What are we to see, Spirit?

PRESENT   Have patience.

(Enter two CHILDREN.)

SONG: "Snow in London"

CHILDREN   Snow – snow –
            Snow falling in London,
            All over London,
            Covering London Town.
            Making ev'ry street lovely and bright for
                              Christmas.
            Somehow snow seems to be right for Christmas.

(Enter CROSSING SWEEPER. He is disgruntled, and remains so throughout the song, to the amusement of the rest.)

SWEEPER   Snow over the City
            Ain't it a pity.

CHILDREN   Oh what a pretty sight.
            Covered with a blanket that makes ev'ry rooftop
            That was grey yesterday suddenly white.

(Enter HOLLY SELLER, and MRS. & MISS GOOD-HEART from opposite sides. They buy holly, then listen, amused.)

SWEEPER   Pity the crossing sweeper
            I've reason to complain,
            Snow just gets deep and deeper
            I sweeps it off again.

ALL   Snow falling in London Mrs. G.H.
            Changing old London

HOLLY S.   Dirty old London Town.
MRS. & MISS   Giving it a new beautiful face for Christmas
HOLLY S.   Like it's wearing a new holiday gown.

MRS. & MISS   Church bells are ringing
CHILDREN   Ringing for Christmas
ALL   From ev'ry steeple
SWEEPER   (spoken - scornfully)   Huh! Merry Christmas!
MRS & MISS   Choirs are singing
CHILDREN   Singing for Christmas
ALL   Telling the people
                  Merry Christmas.

(BOB CRATCHIT, carrying TINY TIM, has entered
during these lines. The CHILDREN start snowballing. BOB joins in.)

ALL   Snowballing in London
                  Snow over London
                  Oh what a wondrous sight.
MRS & MISS   Ev'ry boy and girl has a new game for playing
BOB   Ludgate Hill must have been made for sleighing.
ALL   How faces are glowing
                  Now that it's snowing
TIM   Ev'rywhere growing white
ALL   All the little dark alley ways in the city
                  Now are lit with a new magical light.

SWEEPER   Think of the working classes
                  Snow reaching to our knees
                  Splashed as each carriage passes
                  We just stand here and freeze.

(The rest laugh and jeer at him. He slinks off
still grumbling.)

ALL   Snow falling in London,
                  Changing old London,
                  Dirty old London Town.
                  If we are to make ev'rything right for Christmas
WOMEN   We need snow –
CHILDREN   We need snow –
MEN   We need snow
ALL   Christmas Day.

(The SPIRIT thoroughly enjoys it all, and sprinkles
the participants with silver dust from the torch he
carries. Even SCROOGE becomes animated. As
the song ends, the lights dim out, and a spot lights
SCROOGE and the SPIRIT.)

SCROOGE	Is there a peculiar flavour in what you sprinkle from your torch?
PRESENT	There is. My own. It is the very essence of the Spirit of Christmas.
SCROOGE	Would it apply to any one on this day?
PRESENT	To any with a kindly disposition. To a poor man most.
SCROOGE	Why to a poor man most?
PRESENT	Because he needs it most. But come, we tarry too long. We have much to see this day.
SCROOGE	Where are you taking me now?
PRESENT	To the home of your clerk, Bob Cratchit.
SCROOGE	My clerk!
PRESENT	Come!

They speed across the stage, SCROOGE gamely trying to keep up, and go out R.

Scene 11

CRATCHIT's kitchen. Kitchen range R., with old armchair. Table C. PETER is standing by the fire, fork in hand, in charge of a pan of potatoes. MRS. CRATCHIT is about to put the cloth on the table. BELINDA is jigging about in excitement.

MRS. C.	Come, Belinda, help me lay the table, and do something useful. Don't fuss those potatoes too much, Peter, or they'll never be cooked.
PETER	I'm trying to hurry them, mother. I'm sure they won't be done in time.
MRS. C.	They will if you leave them alone. Whatever can have got your precious father and Tiny Tim? Church must have been over long ago. And Martha warn't as late last Christmas Day by half an hour.

(Small BOY and GIRL rush in and dance round their mother.)

BOY	The goose, the goose, I can smell the goose!
GIRL	Is it ready, mother, is it ready yet, is it time for dinner?

MRS. C.	Now quiet both of you. It's not ready by an hour, and your father isn't home from church yet.
BOY	Peter's doing the tatoes, Peter's doing the tatoes.
GIRL	Can you cook, Peter? Will they be all right?
PETER	Course they'll be all right. I'm doing them.
BELINDA	Here comes Martha, mother.
BOY & GIRL	Here comes Martha, mother. There's such a goose, Martha.

(They run over to greet her as MARTHA enters. She is the eldest child, in her teens.)

MARTHA	Here comes Martha, mother. Lor', what excitement. (She takes off her bonnet and shawl.)
MRS. C.	Why, bless your heart alive, my dear, how late you are. (She kisses her and takes the bonnet and shawl.) Surely you were not still sewing dresses for the ladies on Christmas morning?
MARTHA	We'd a deal of work to finish up last night, mother, and had to clear away this morning.
MRS. C.	Well, never mind so long as you are come. Sit ye down by the fire and warm yourself, my dear.
BOY	Come and smell the goose, Martha, it's cooking in the oven.
MRS. C.	Now, let her be. Poor Martha is tired.
MARTHA	I'm all right, mother.
GIRL	There's father coming. Hide, Martha, hide.
BOY	Hide here, Martha.

(She hides U.S. of fireplace. There is much giggling as BOB enters, carrying TINY TIM on his shoulder. The CHILDREN all run to him, saying "Hello father" and "Hello Tim".)

BOB	Hello, hello, hello. (He puts TIM down and looks round.) Why, where's our Martha?
MRS. C.	(mock sad) Not coming.
BOB	Not coming? Not coming on Christmas Day?

(MARTHA then runs out from her hiding place into his arms. The CHILDREN laugh and dance round.)

MARTHA   Of course I'm here on Christmas Day, dear father.

GIRL   She was hiding!

BOY   Lift me up, father.

            (BOB tosses him into the air.)

GIRL   And me, and me. My turn now.   (She has her
            turn.)

BELINDA   Tim, the goose is nearly done. Can you smell it
            cooking?

TIM   I can, I can. It must be a mighty goose.

PETER   And I'm watching the potatoes!

BOB   They'll be the best potatoes ever, I'll be bound.

BOY   Let's go and listen to the pudding singing in the
            copper.

GIRL   Yes, let's. Come on, Tim.

            (All the CHILDREN go out except MARTHA.)

MRS. C.   And how did little Tim behave?

BOB   (unwinding his scarf, which Martha takes)   As
            good as gold, and better. Somehow he gets thought-
            ful sitting by himself so much, and he thinks the
            strangest things you ever heard. He told me coming
            home that he hoped the people might see him in church
            because he was a cripple, and it might be pleasant
            to them to remember on Christmas Day who it was
            made lame beggars walk and blind men see.

MRS. C.   (touched, and comforted by MARTHA)   Did he?
            Did he really?

BOB   And d'you know, my dear, I do believe he's getting
            stronger.

MRS. C.   I'm sure he is, I'm sure he is.   (She blows her
            nose.)

            (Enter all the CHILDREN.)

BELINDA   The pudding is boiling in the copper, mother, and it
            smells as though it must be done.

PETER   Yes, it must be done.

MRS. C.   Well, it can't be far off now, it's been boiling since
            before you were awake this morning. But I'll tell

you what we'll do. The goose is ready for basting, so we'll take him out and have a quick look.

CHILDREN   Hurrah! The goose!

(MRS. CRATCHIT takes the goose from the side oven, and puts it on the table. It is a tiny bird.)

MRS. C.   Now, we can all take it in turns to baste if we are quick. You first, Tim.

(They hand the spoon from one to another, amid great excitement and acclamations. Last one is BOB.)

BOB   I declare I have never seen a bird the like of this one. It is a very giant of a goose, fit for a king.

MRS. C.   Now, back into the oven to finish off before it gets cold.

BOB   Yes, it mustn't get cold. It might get goose pimples.

(The CHILDREN laugh. The goose is returned to the oven.)

Now I must make my Christmas punch. Hand me the kettle from the hob, Martha.   (He places a bowl on the table, and pours on water from the kettle.)

BOY   Can we all have some, father?

BOB   Of course we can. We must drink a toast. Bring me the glasses, Peter, do.   (He pours the liquid into a jug.)

GIRL   Can't I bring the glasses?

BOB   No, this is a special day for Peter.

MRS. C.   A special day for Peter? What is it then, my dear?

ALL   What is it, father? Please tell us.

BOB   We have a surprise, haven't we, Tim?

(TIM nods vigorously.)

Quiet everyone, and I'll tell you. I think I have found a situation for you, Peter.

BOY   Ooh, Peter's going to work.

GIRL   You're grown up, Peter.

MRS. C.   Bless you, my dear.

MARTHA   You'll be a real man of business, I'm sure.

BOB   Well, at twelve years old it's time you were making
              your way in the world, not hanging about the house
              with your mother.

MRS. C.   Oh, really, he's just a child still.

BOB   And this situation will bring in no less than five
              and six a week.

              (General chorus of "Oohs".)

              Congratulations, my boy.

PETER   Thank you, father.   (They shake hands solemnly.)

BOB   Now we'll drink a toast to Peter.

              (The glasses are filled, and they all drink to
              PETER.)

TIM   Can I give a toast?

BOB   Why, of course you can. All quiet for a toast
              from Tim.

              (They help TIM up on to the chair, where he is
              supported by BOB.)

TIM   SONG: "A Christmas Carol"

                    Here's a toast for Christmas Day
                    My toast for Christmas Day
                    Here's to those we love the dearest
                    May they prosper through the year
                    Never shed a tear
                    Be joyful everyone.

                    May the people
                    Who are not so blessed as we
                    Find contentment
                    Each in his own special way
                    Upon this Christmas Day

                    Gentle Jesus born this day
                    Made it holy for alway
                    As he blessed that lowly stable
                    May he bless our home today
                    Keep us safe we pray
                    God bless us everyone.

              (Repeat with all CHILDREN singing in unison, but
              in the last stanza they take a line each, the last

line being taken by TINY TIM. They all applaud as the song ends, and TIM is helped down.)

BOB   I'll give you a toast. Mr. Scrooge. I give you Mr. Scrooge, the founder of the feast.

MRS. C.   The founder of the feast indeed! I wish I had him here. I'd give him a piece of my mind to feast upon and I hope he'd have a good appetite for it.

BOB   My dear, the children. Christmas Day.

MRS. C.   It should be Christmas Day I'm sure, on which one drinks the health of such an odious, stingy, hard, unfeeling man as Mr. Scrooge. You know he is, Robert; nobody knows it better than you do.

BOB   My dear, Christmas Day.

MRS. C.   I'll drink his health for your sake, and the day's, not for his. Long life to him, a merry Christmas, and a happy New Year. He'll be very merry and very happy, I have no doubt.

             (They all drink SCROOGE's health, but quietly and without enthusiasm.)

BELINDA   Father, please will you tell us a story?

CHILDREN   Yes, a story. A Christmas story.

             (BOB sits in the chair. The CHILDREN group round him. During the song MRS. CRATCHIT and MARTHA busy themselves with the final preparations for dinner: the table, the potatoes, and finally, the goose from the oven.)

             SONG: "A Story"

BOB   I'll tell you a tale of a goose
             It was the farmyard's pride
             But the silly bird was quite absurd
             And longed for the world outside.
             He said "I've got a wanderlust
             I feel my feet are itchin' "
             Next thing he knew he found himself
             Inside Bob Cratchit's kitchen.

CHILDREN   Hurrah, what a story, a really splendid story,
             And every word
             That we have heard
             Is absolutely true
             Tell us another one do.

BOB   I'll tell you a tale of a pud
               A jolly Christmas Pud.
               He was a beaut, all stuffed with fruit
               And everything that's good.
               He wore a coat of custard
               And I heard him say "Oh lumme"
               Next thing he knew he found himself
               Inside Bob Cratchit's tummy.

CHILDREN   Hurrah, what a story – etc.

BOB   I'll tell you a tale of a boy
               A boy called Tiny Tim
               Who then ere long grew big and strong
               And sound in every limb.
               They say he joined the Navy
               And went round the world cavortin'
               Then came back home to Cratchit's house
               When he had made his fortune.

CHILDREN   Hurrah, what a story, a really splendid story,
               And every word that we have heard
               Is absolutely true
               And no one tells a story half as well as you.

               At the end of the song the white tabs close amid
               gales of laughter.

Scene 12

SCROOGE   Spirit, tell me if Tiny Tim will live.

PRESENT   I see a vacant seat in the poor chimney corner,
               and a crutch without an owner.

SCROOGE   Oh no, no, no. Kind Spirit, say he will be spared.

PRESENT   If these shadows remain unaltered by the future,
               the child will die. What then? If he be like to die
               he had better do it, and help decrease the surplus
               population.

SCROOGE   (penitent)   Oh dear, oh dear.

PRESENT   The words seem familiar to you?

SCROOGE   They are my words, Spirit. I uttered them.   But
               how I wish I could retract them now.

PRESENT   It would seem then that you are learning something
               from what I am showing you. But come. Your name
               is being mentioned under another roof this day.

They speed off the stage as the lights dim, tabs
open, and lights up on:

Scene 13

SCROOGE   Why, that is my nephew – how quickly you travel,
            Spirit. And his wife. And who are the other two?

            (The scene is FRED's parlour. FRED, his WIFE,
            his WIFE's SISTER and TOPPER sit round a
            table covered in a velvet cloth. They each have a
            glass in front of them. It is clearly after dinner.
            As the scene opens FRED is roaring with laughter.
            He is a man who laughs constantly and infectiously.
            They all join in his laughing.)

FRED   Humbug, he said. He said that Christmas was a
            humbug, as I live. And he believed it too. What
            do you say to that, my dear?

WIFE   More shame on him, husband.

FRED   He's a comical old fellow, and not so pleasant as
            he might be. But his offences carry their own
            punishment, and I have really nothing against him.

GIRL   But haven't you always said that he is very rich?

FRED   What of that? His wealth is of no use to him. He
            doesn't make himself comfortable with it. And he
            hasn't even the satisfaction of thinking that he is
            ever going to benefit us with it.   (He laughs
            again.)

WIFE   Oh, I have no patience with him.

TOPPER   And neither have I.   I think he must enjoy his
            wretchedness.

FRED   Oh, come now. I couldn't be angry with him if I
            tried. Who suffers most from his ill humours?
            Himself always. He takes it into his head to dis-
            like us and he won't come and dine with us. What's
            the consequence? He don't miss much of a dinner.
            (More laughs.)

WIFE   Oh, he don't, don't he? I think he misses a very
            good dinner.

FRED   Well, I'm very glad to hear you say so for I have
            no great faith in these young housekeepers. What
            do you say, Topper?

WIFE   )
GIRL   )   (together)   Well!
)   Oh, Fred!

TOPPER   Who am I to judge? I'm only a wretched outcast of
               a bachelor. Find me a wife and I will be able to
               express an opinion on the subject of housekeeping.

               (The GIRL is blushing at this exchange, while
               FRED laughs and digs everyone in the ribs.)

GIRL   I think you are very unkind and ungrateful, Fred.
               If I were your wife I would be hurt by your joking.
               I can't remember when I enjoyed a Christmas dinner
               more.

TOPPER   Hear, hear.

FRED   Ha, ha, ha; no, of course, it was a magnificent
               dinner.   (Sings.)

               SONG   "A Lady Who Can Cook"

                  I must confess, my dear, I'm a very lucky man
                  To have a wife as talented as you are.
                  For pretty girls are plentiful, and seen on
                                            ev'ry hand,
                  But useful ones are relatively fewer.
                  So Topper, let me offer this advice,
                  Before you go a'courting, just think twice.

                  When you're searching for a partner who can
                                    share your married bliss,
                  Don't consider how attractive she may look.
                  And before you even try to steal that compromising
                                            kiss
                  Make absolutely certain she can cook.
                  Though she may be fair of countenance and full
                                            of female grace
                  And you're very keen to get her on the hook,
                  There's a limit to the time you can enjoy a
                                            pretty face
                  But you'll always love a lady who can cook.

ALL   Who can cook – who can cook.
FRED   It's a necessary attribute you cannot overlook.
ALL   Who can cook – who can cook.
               You will always love a lady who can cook.

TOPPER   But it's really very difficult when looking for a
                                    wife,

	And you meet perchance in some secluded nook.
	Before you ask the question that will make her yours for life
	To say "Madam, please be mine – if you can cook."
WIFE	But Topper, do be practical, and keep this thought in mind,
	There will come a time when youth has been forsook,
	And the pleasures that you treasure are the culinary kind –
	You'll be grateful for a lady who can cook.
ALL	Who can cook – who can cook.
	It's a necessary attribute you cannot overlook.
	Who can cook – who can cook.
	You will always love a lady who can cook.
GIRL	I don't want to be presumptuous, but since you haven't asked
	You really haven't very far to look.
	If you're seeking creature comforts I am equal to the task,
	And I'm absolutely splendid as a cook.
ALL	She can cook – she can cook.
	It's a necessary attribute you cannot overlook.
	She can cook –
GIRL	I can cook!
ALL	You will always love a lady
FRED	Who will bring you home the gravy
ALL	You will always love a lady who can cook.

(After the song there is general laughter.)

FRED   What we need is some exercise.

(Moans.)

We ought to play a game.

(Cries of pleasure.)

GIRL   Oh, yes, Fred. What shall we play?

FRED   (slyly)   How about forfeits, eh, Topper?

(They laugh at the GIRL's discomfiture.)

WIFE   I know. We shall play hunt the thimble.

(General approval.)

I will get a thimble, and you can start, my dear.

FRED   Excellent. Come, all out of the room.

          (FRED, WIFE and TOPPER go out, while the
          GIRL flits to and fro looking for a hiding place.
          SCROOGE has been thoroughly enjoying the party,
          and is childishly pleased at the prospect of a game.)

SCROOGE   Oh, how I would like to play this game with them.
          Do you think I could join in, Spirit? After all,
          Fred is my nephew, my sister's child.

PRESENT   Join in? Man, you are but a shadow, a wraith.
          Although you are privileged to look upon this gay
          party by my intercession, they can neither see you
          nor hear you. In any event, if they had wanted you
          here they would have invited you.

SCROOGE   But I <u>was</u> invited, Spirit.

PRESENT   And you refused.

          (SCROOGE hangs his head. The GIRL has now
          hidden the thimble behind the curtains. She skips
          to the centre.)

GIRL   I'm ready.

          (Enter FRED, WIFE and TOPPER.)

FRED   So the hunt is on. Tantivy!

          (They all begin searching.)

TOPPER   I'm sure you have made it so difficult that we shall
          never find it.

WIFE   I shall use a woman's intuition to find it. Am I
          getting warm?

SCROOGE   (excited)   No, you are very cold.

WIFE   Well, am I?

GIRL   No, you are very cold.

FRED   This is a most artful thimble hider. I think you have
          played this game before.

SCROOGE   Topper is getting very warm.

TOPPER   Am I getting warm?

GIRL   Well –

SCROOGE   It's behind the curtain, Topper, behind the curtain!

TOPPER	(finding it) I have it. Behind the curtain!
FRED	Well, there's a thing. The man must have super-natural powers.
TOPPER	Don't I get a reward?
WIFE	Topper! Remember we are not playing forfeits! (They all laugh.)
PRESENT	Come, my time is growing short. It is time we journeyed on.
SCROOGE	Oh, Spirit, can we not stay until the end of the party?
PRESENT	That cannot be.
SCROOGE	Well, just for one more game then, just one more.
PRESENT	I cannot deny you that. I relent for one more game,
FRED	I have it. We will play a game of Yes and No.
WIFE	I've never heard of it. I believe you have just made it up.
FRED	No, no. It's a splendid game. I will think of something, and you must all ask me questions to discover what it is. But I can only answer yes or no.
TOPPER	Oh, yes, this is a good game. Have you thought of something, Fred?
FRED	(mock thinking) Ye-es. (He bursts out laughing. Yes, I have indeed. Open fire with your broadsides. (They all sit down but FRED, who paces about as he answers the questions. Although he can only answer yes or no, his answers are full of expression and he laughs intemperately.)
WIFE	Is it an animal?
FRED	Yes.
GIRL	A live animal?
FRED	Yes.
TOPPER	A friendly animal?
FRED	No.
GIRL	A disagreeable animal?

FRED	Yes.
WIFE	Is it a savage animal?
FRED	Yes.
WIFE	A tiger?
FRED	No.
TOPPER	Can we see it in London?
FRED	Yes.
GIRL	Does it walk in the streets?
FRED	Yes.
SCROOGE	Is it a horse?
WIFE	Is it a horse?
FRED	No.
SCROOGE	Is it in a menagerie?
TOPPER	Is it in a menagerie?
FRED	No.
SCROOGE	Is it ever killed in the market?
GIRL	Is it ever killed in the market?
FRED	I doubt not.
SCROOGE	Does it grunt and growl?
WIFE	Does it grunt and growl?
FRED	No. Yes, I mean yes.
WIFE	A pig? A cow?
TOPPER	A bull? A dog?
GIRL	An ass? A donkey?
SCROOGE	A cat? A bear?
WIFE	A bear?
FRED	(rolling with laughter) No. No. No. No. No.
GIRL	I have it. I know what it is. It's your Uncle Scrooge!
FRED	You're right, you're right. It's my Uncle Scrooge.
WIFE	Well, that's not fair. It was a bear.

TOPPER   And an ass.

            (They all join in the laughter.)

FRED   He has given us plenty of merriment, I'm sure, and
            it would be ungrateful not to drink his health. Let
            us drink to our declining guest. I give you –
            Uncle Scrooge.

ALL   Uncle Scrooge.

FRED   A merry Christmas and a happy New Year to the
            old man, wherever he is. He wouldn't take it from
            me, but he shall have it none the less. Uncle
            Scrooge.

            They all dissolve into laughter again as they clink
            glasses in the toast. The lights fade on the scene;
            the white tabs close.

Scene 14

            SCROOGE and the SPIRIT OF CHRISTMAS
            PRESENT are spotlit C.

SCROOGE   (chuckling)   That was a splendid game. A bear.
            He he!

PRESENT   And such a merry scene is re-enacted everywhere
            when the Spirit of Christmas is abroad. Wherever
            there is a generous, open heart, there I leave my
            blessing.   (Yawns hugely.)

SCROOGE   You are tired, Spirit, and you are grown older.

PRESENT   I am. My life upon this globe is very brief.

SCROOGE   Are Spirit lives so short?

SPIRIT   Mine ends tonight at midnight. Hark, the time is
            drawing near.

            (Chimes of three-quarter hour. There is a move-
            ment behind the SPIRIT's cloak.)

SCROOGE   Forgive me for what I ask, but do I see a claw
            reaching from your cloak?

PRESENT   It might well be a claw for all the flesh there is
            upon it. Look here.

            (He brings out from under his cloak two thin WAIFS.
            They are dirty, emaciated, and wearing only rags.
            Shivering, they cling to his cloak and stare at

SCROOGE.)

SCROOGE	(starting back, appalled) Spirit, are they yours?
PRESENT	Mine? They are Man's. They are Man's. They cling to me, appeal-ing to me to save them from their lot. This boy is Ignorance, and this girl is Want. Beware them both, and all of their degree. But most of all beware this boy, for on his brow I see that written which is Doom, unless the writing be erased.
SCROOGE	Have they no refuge or resource?

(Music starts: Reprise. "Christmas is Humbug")

PRESENT	Are there no prisons?
SCROOGE	Oh, no!
PRESENT	Are there no workhouses?
SCROOGE	I can't bear it.
PRESENT	Have the Tread Mill and the Poor Law ceased to function?
SCROOGE	Have mercy on me, Spirit.
PRESENT	You consigned them there without the least com-punction. By what logic do you show compassion now?
SCROOGE	I said these things before I was so wise but now the scales are falling from my eyes.
PRESENT	Charity is Humbug your words were plain to hear. You said the idle suffer from starvation. If they want to die of hunger, who are you to inter- fere - It will help decrease the surplus population. And these two are the innocents you hurry to condemn Without the slightest knowledge of their worth.

Before you sit in judgment on your hapless fellow
men
You must recognise the surplus
Is it you or they who're worthless?
And perhaps you'll find a purpose here on earth.
Pray for forgiveness
Pray for forgiveness
On your knees.

During these last lines, the chimes of a clock ring

out. SCROOGE is kneeling, penitent, weeping.
As the first stroke of twelve sounds, the SPIRIT
and CHILDREN fade, and only SCROOGE is dimly
lit. The gauze closes, the white tabs open, and as
the last stroke of twelve is heard we see the
macabre figure of CHRISTMAS FUTURE lit behind
the gauze. He is like the figure of Death, dressed
all in black, with a black veil over his face.

Scene 15

SCROOGE raises his head.

SCROOGE   Twelve. The stroke of twelve. The Spirit of
Christmas Present has left me, but what did
Marley say? Expect the third Spirit when the
last stroke of twelve has ceased to vibrate. I
feel a presence now. I dare not look.

(He begins to shiver violently, and slowly looks
round. He sees the SPIRIT and gives a horrified
cry. The SPIRIT remains motionless, pointing a
long finger at him. He rises slowly to his feet.)

I am in the presence of the Ghost of Christmas Yet
to Come?

(The SPIRIT does not move, and continues pointing.)

You are about to show me the shadows of the things
that have not yet happened, but will happen in the
time before us. Is that so, Spirit?

(The SPIRIT lowers its arm and inclines its head.)

Ghost of the Future, I fear you more than any
spectre I have seen, but as I know your purpose
is to do me good, I will bear you company, and do
it with a thankful heart. Will you not speak to me?

(The SPIRIT again extends a long arm, and slowly
beckons.)

Lead on, lead on, the night is waning fast, and it
is precious time to me I know. Lead on, Spirit.

(They both go out L. The gauze has risen, and a
light comes up R., revealing HOLLY SELLER
and POULTERER.)

HOLLY S.   'Ere, have you heard the news?

POULT.   The news? Yes, man, 'tis Christmas morning,

and you'll sell no more of your holly for twelve
long months.

HOLLY S.   No, no. This is real news.

SONG: "He's Dead"

           He's dead.
POULT.   Dead?
HOLLY S.   He's dead.
POULT.   Who's dead?
HOLLY S.   Ole skinflint, he's dead.
POULT.   No!
HOLLY S.   They found him there this morning
           In his old fourposter bed.
           Not a soul to mourn his passing
POULT.   Not a tear will be shed.
BOTH   On account of Ole Skinflint is dead.

(Enter JOE.)

POULT.   He's gorn.
JOE   Gorn?
HOLLY S.   He's gorn.
JOE   Who's gorn?
P. & H.   Ole Skinflint, he's gorn.
JOE   No!
P. & H.   There's many a man in London
           Who will hail this happy morn.
JOE   And not a yard of veiling will be taken out of
                                    pawn
ALL   On account of Ole Skinflint is gorn.
JOE   Oh, it's wrong to speak ill of the departed,
           It's recognised to be a wicked sin.
POULT.   But can any one pretend he's brokenhearted
           When the world will be a better place without
                                    him in!
ALL   He's dead, he's dead, Ole Skinflint is dead.
           There are things we know about him that are
                              better left unsaid.
POULT.   He's gone up to his Maker
HOLLY S.   Or the other place instead.
ALL   On account of Ole Skinflint is dead.

(They do a little dance, and then:)

ALL   He's dead, he's dead, Ole Skinflint is dead
JOE   And who'll be at his funeral to walk with
                                solemn tread?

POULT.   I wouldn't mind attendin', if you're sure that
                                        we'll be fed
ALL   On account of Ole Skinflint is dead.
                He's gorn, he's gorn, Ole Skinflint is gorn,
HOLLY S.   For all the good he's been here he had better
                                        not been born.
JOE   With his last account to settle, and it's badly
                                        overdrawn
ALL   On account of Ole Skinflint is gorn.
                (Mock solemn.)
                Oh, it's wrong to speak ill of the departed
                It's recognised to be a wicked sin.
                But can anyone pretend he's brokenhearted
                When the world will be a better place without
                                        him in.
                He's dead, he's dead, Ole Skinflint is dead.
POULT.   No more widows for eviction
HOLLY L.   No more debtors to be bled
ALL   Now he'll have to start atoning for the wicked
                                        life he led
                On account of Ole Skinflint is dead.

                (As the song ends there is much laughter and
                gaiety. HOLLY SELLER and POULTERER go out
                R., and JOE turns to go into his shop through the
                door C. As he does so MRS. DILBER enters R.,
                carrying a large bundle.)

MRS. D.   Joe. Joe, I was just a-comin' to see you. I've a
                few bits 'ere that might take your fancy.

JOE   Oh, it's you, Mrs. Dilber. I thought as 'ow I might
                be 'aving the pleasure of your company afore long.

MRS. D.   You did?

JOE   I did. You're 'otfoot from old Scratch's, I'll be
                bound. And you 'aven't wasted no time about it.

MRS. D.   You've 'eard, then.

JOE   Oh, yes, I've 'eard. 'E breathed 'is last this very
                morning.

MRS. D.   Well, ain't I 'is laundress, then? Ain't it only
                right as I should 'ave first pickings?

JOE   Come into my parlour, Mrs. Dilber, come into my
                parlour.

                (They go through the door into the shop L.)

Now let's see what you've acquired, Mrs. Dilber.

(He turns up his lamp, and begins to open the bundle. As he does so, a CHARWOMAN enters R. with another large bundle. She goes over to JOE's door, and stands outside listening.)

A couple of sheets, eh? Well used, I'd say.

MRS. D.   They're 'ardly touched, you old scoundrel. You're worse nor what 'e was.

JOE   And a towel. Past its best. I can't give you much for that, Mrs. Dilber.

(CHARWOMAN bursts into the shop. During the following exchange JOE smokes his clay pipe.)

CHAR   So you got 'ere first, did you?

MRS. D.   Well, look who's 'ere. Where d'you think she's been this morning, eh Joe?

CHAR   What odds then? What odds, Mrs. Dilber? Every person 'as a right to take care o' themselves. 'E always did.

MRS. D.   That's true indeed. No man more so.

CHAR   Well then, that's enough. Who's the worse for the loss of a few things like these. Not a dead man, I suppose?

MRS. D.   No, indeed.

CHAR   If 'e wanted to keep 'em after 'e was dead, the wicked old screw, 'e should 'ave been a bit more natural in 'is life time. Then 'e'd 'ave 'ad somebody to look after 'im when 'e was struck down, instead of lying gasping out 'is last there, alone by 'imself.

MRS. D.   It's the truest word ever was spoke. It's a judgement on 'im. That's what it is, a judgement.

CHAR   It would 'ave been a sight 'eavier judgement if I could 'ave laid my 'ands on anything else, you may depend on it. Come on, old Joe, finish off Mrs. Dilber's bundle and let's start on mine. We know pretty well that we was all 'elping ourselves afore we met 'ere. I ain't ashamed. It's no sin.

JOE   Very well, ladies. Let's see what else we 'ave.

A pair of silver spoons. Mmm – sugar tongs – and the gentleman's boots, to be sure.

MRS. D.   'Is best boots, I'll 'ave you know. 'Is best boots, not 'is everyday ones.

JOE   To be sure.   (He ruminates for a moment.) I'll give you five shilling for the lot.

MRS. D.   (affronted)   Five shilling!

JOE   That's your account, and I wouldn't give you another sixpence if I was to be boiled for not doing it.

MRS. D.   Why, it's worth 'alf a sovereign if it's worth an 'alfpenny.

JOE   Five shilling is too much. I always give too much to the ladies. It's a weakness of mine, and that's the way I ruin myself. That's your account. If you asked me for another penny I'd repent of being so liberal and knock off 'alf a crown.

(MRS. DILBER grumbles to herself.)

CHAR   And now undo my bundle, Joe.

(He does, and takes out the bed curtains from SCROOGE's bed.)

JOE   What d'you call this? Bed curtains?

CHAR   Aha. Bed curtains.   (She cackles.)

JOE   You don't mean to say you took 'em down, rings an' all, with 'im lying there?

CHAR   Yes, I do. And why not?

JOE   You was born to make your fortune, you was, an' I'll wager you'll do it.

CHAR   I certainly shan't stay my 'and when I can get something in it by reaching it out, for the sake of such a man as 'e was, I promise you.

(JOE is holding up an old blanket.)

Don't drop your tobaccer over that blanket now.

JOE   His blanket?

CHAR   Whose else? 'E isn' likely to take cold without 'em, I dare say.

JOE   I 'ope 'e didn't die of anything catching.

CHAR   Don't be afraid o' that. I'm not so fond of 'is company that I'd loiter about 'im for such things if 'e did.

(JOE has picked out a shirt.)

And you'll not find an 'ole on that shirt. It was 'is best. They'd 'ave wasted it but for me.

JOE   What do you call wasting it?

CHAR   Putting it on 'im to be buried in. Somebody was fool enough to do it, but I took it off again. (Cackles.) Calico is quite as becoming to the body, and 'e can't look no uglier than 'e did in that one.

JOE   You're a 'ard one, an' no mistake. But you've an eye for a bargain. I'll give you seven shilling for it all.

MRS. D.   'Ere!

CHAR   An' I'll take it, Joe. There's a drop or two o' gin in that, Mrs. Dilber, eh? Pay up, old Joe.

(JOE reaches in a canvas bag, and fishes out some coins, which he counts slowly into their hands.)

So there's the end on't, d'you see. 'E frightened everyone away from 'im when 'e was alive, to profit us when 'e was dead!

They all collapse into cackling laughter. The lights fade, and the gauze closes.

Scene 16

SCROOGE and the SPIRIT are spotlit in front of gauze.

SCROOGE   Spirit, this is a fearful place. Bear me away from it. I beseech you. I see the fate of this unhappy man could be my own. My life tends that way now. But spare me more of it. In leaving I shall not leave the lesson, trust me.

(The SPIRIT remains immobile. SCROOGE waits for a moment, twisting his hands.)

Good Spirit, speak. Speak and tell me that these things which we see are the shadows only of the things that may be, not the things that will be.

Men's courses will foreshadow certain ends, to which they must lead. But surely if the courses be departed from, the ends will change. Say it is thus with what you show me.

The SPIRIT raises his hand and points. SCROOGE' gaze fearfully follows. The spot on them fades as the lights come up on:

Scene 17

Two gravestones C., one small, one large. As the lights go up, BOB CRATCHIT is seen kneeling by the small gravestone. His small son and daughter enter hand in hand. The girl is carrying a posy of flowers. They kneel beside their father and place the flowers on the grave.

BOB   Come, come children. We must be getting home or your mother will be worrying about us.

BOY   Yes, father.

GIRL   Goodbye, Tim.

BOY   Goodbye, Tim.

             SONG: "Tiny Tim"

CHILDREN   Tiny Tim, Tiny Tim,
                 You couldn't help loving him
                 Always happy and cheerful
                 Never a tear for the pain he was in.
                 Tiny Tim, Tiny Tim,
                 We'll always remember him.
BOB   No one could wish for a better son
                 Home is dull now he's gone
CHILDREN   God bless us everyone
                 Said Tiny Tim.

                 Tiny Tim, Tiny Tim,
BOB   You couldn't help loving him.
                 Always thoughtful for others
CHILDREN   Kindest of brothers there ever has been.
                 Tiny Tim, Tiny Tim,
                 We'll always remember him.
                 When he was with us we all had fun
                 And the sun always shone
                 God bless us everyone
                 Said Tiny Tim.

             (BOB leads the two CHILDREN gently away. They

go out R. , and the lights fade on that side of the
stage. Lights up on SCROOGE and SPIRIT L.)

SCROOGE   Oh Spirit, what a very sad scene that was. Did
Tiny Tim have to die? Could nothing be done to
save him?

(The SPIRIT points toward the larger gravestone.)

What is it you wish me to do?

(The SPIRIT still points.)

You wish me to look at the other grave. To read
what is written upon the stone? Spirit, I am fearful
to do it. I cannot look.

(The SPIRIT still points, and SCROOGE approaches
the stone slowly, reads it, and falls back with a cry,
covering his face with his hands.)

Ebenezer Scrooge! It is my grave! I am the man
whose clothes they were selling. I am the man whose
death brought pleasure to those people. No, Spirit,
no, no, no. Hear me.   (He falls upon his knees.)
I am not the man I was. I am not the man I would
have been but for this meeting. Why show me all
this if I am past all hope? Pity me, and tell me that
I may yet change these shadows you have shown me
by an altered life.   (He clutches at the SPIRIT's
robe.)   I will honour Christmas in my heart, and
try to keep it all the year. Oh, tell me I may sponge
away the writing on the stone.

He falls weeping to the ground, still clutching the
robe, from which the SPIRIT has now vanished.
During this last speech the lights have faded on the
gravestones, and the whole stage has dimmed to
permit the transformation to:

Scene 18

SCROOGE's room. SCROOGE is still upon the
floor sobbing, and holding the black shroud from the
last SPIRIT. As the lights come up he raises himself and looks around him.

SCROOGE   My room. And my bed.   (He hurries over to it.)
They are not torn down. They are not torn down,
rings and all. They are here. I am here. It was
all a dream.   (He looks down at the shroud on his

hand.)   But the Spirits were real enough.   The three Spirits just as Jacob Marley foretold.   (He throws the shroud on the bed.)   Oh, Jacob Marley, Heaven be praised.   Thankee, Jacob, thankee for the warning you gave me.   (Sings.)

> Jacob Marley was a fine man of business
> The truest friend a man could wish to have.

(Spoken.)   O, there's much to be done this day, and little enough time to do it in.   (He begins to get dressed.)   I must hurry with my dressing. (Sings.)

> The warning that he gave me was a timely one
> I shall heed it, Jacob, that you may depend.
> Tho' the method of his telling came as something
>   of a shock,
> Jacob Marley is a good and honest friend.

(Spoken.)   I don't even know what day of the month it is. I don't know how long I have been amongst the spirits.   (He goes over to the window and throws it open. There is a sound of bells ringing.)   Why, the street is full of people – and what a day! All frost and sunshine. I wonder what day it is. I'll ask the boy down there. He looks a pleasant intelligent fellow. Boy! Hey, you down there. Boy!

BOY (off)   'Allo.

SCROOGE (sings)   What's today, my fine fellow?

BOY Why, today is Christmas Day.

SCROOGE Today is Christmas Day, I haven't missed it.
The Spirits must have done it in one night,
But of course they can do anything they like,
Of course they can, of course they can.
Listen boy.

BOY Yeah.

SCROOGE Do you chance to know the poulterer
At the bottom of Cornhill?

BOY O' course I do.

SCROOGE He's got a massive turkey in the window
The biggest bird that you will ever see.
Go and tell him that it must be kept for me.

BOY Garn!

SCROOGE   There's half a crown for you if you agree.

BOY   Righto, Guvner, I'm off!

(SCROOGE comes D.S. as he sings, finishing dressing and putting on coat and hat. He is lit by a spot, and the rest of the lights dim so that the scene can be changed from SCROOGE's room to the same street scene as Scene I.)

SCROOGE   I shall buy Norfolk Turkey
                 And that fine Norfolk Turkey
                 Will be my Norfolk Turkey before long.
                 Then I'll make it a present
                 To my clerk, oh how pleasant
                 It's a gift that can't go wrong.
                 And I'll send it down
                 To Camden Town
                 How puzzled all the Cratchits will be
                 To receive it thus
                 Anonymous
                 But none the less they'll never guess
                 That it was sent from me.
                 They'll feast their eyes on this Turkey
                 What a size is this Turkey
                 It's the prize Norfolk Turkey to appear
                 There's no one more deserving for
                 The prize Norfolk Turkey this year.

The lights go up on the street scene. The POULT-ERER is at his shop, with the Turkey in his hand. He is talking to the BOY. Two other CHILDREN are there, the HOLLY SELLER, a GENT. and a LADY as in Scene I.

Scene 19

ALL   Come and buy Norfolk Turkey
                 You should try Norfolk Turkey
POULT   Only my Norfolk Turkeys are the best.
ALL   See this fine Norfolk Turkey
                 It's a prime Norfolk Turkey
                 With a plump and tender breast.

(During the next eight bars SCROOGE buys the Turkey, pays the POULTERER, and despatches the BOY to Camden Town.)

                 If you want a goose, they're here to choose
                 No gander could be grander than these

If you fancy duck, then you're in luck
They're fresh today from Aylesbury
And guaranteed to please.
Feast your eyes on this Turkey
What a size is this Turkey
It's the prize Norfolk Turkey of the year
All succulent for this rich gent
The prize Norfolk Turkey

SCROOGE   A surprise Norfolk Turkey

ALL   The prize Norfolk Turkey is here.

POULT.   Now don't you worry, sir, it'll be with Mr. Cratchit in plenty of time for his dinner.

SCROOGE   And he must never know who sent it.

POULT.   My lips is sealed!

SCROOGE   What a capital joke!

(CRATCHIT enters with TINY TIM on his shoulder. They are dancing along and laughing. They barge into the back of SCROOGE. He swirls round.)

Cratchit!

BOB   Mr. Scrooge, sir, I – I'm very sorry, sir, indeed I am, I didn't mean – I – I –

SCROOGE   A Merry Christmas, Bob.   (Claps him on the back.)

BOB   I – I beg pardon –

SCROOGE   A Merrier Christmas, Bob, my good fellow, than I have given you for many a year.

BOB   And a Merry Christmas to you, Mr. Scrooge, sir, to be sure.

SCROOGE   And I suppose this is Tiny Tim.

BOB   Well, yes, Mr. Scrooge, but how did you know – ?

SCROOGE   You should have told me about him before, Bob. Hello, Tim.

TIM   Hello Mr. Scrooge. You're a nice man. My mother said that –

BOB   Tim! That's enough.

SCROOGE   Bob, I'm glad that we met. We will discuss your affairs when you come into the office tomorrow, but I have decided to raise your salary, and to endeavour to assist your struggling family, especially Tiny Tim here.

BOB   Are you feeling quite well, Mr. Scrooge?

SCROOGE   Never better, thankee Bob. And Bob. We must really buy a bigger coal scuttle.

BOB   I think I ought to fetch Mr. Fred.

(He goes off with TINY TIM.)

HOLLY S.   Holly, holly, who'll buy my holly!

SCROOGE   Here, my good man, I'll buy your holly. Yes, holly is just what I need.

HOLLY S.   Thankee kindly, sir.

(As the transaction takes place, MRS. GOODHEART and her daughter cross L. to R. SCROOGE sees them, comes towards them and they meet D.C.)

SCROOGE   My dear madam, how do you do? I hope you had a successful day for your charity yesterday. It was kind of you to call on me. A Merry Christmas to you, ma'am.

MRS. G.   (very haughty)   Mr. Scrooge.

SCROOGE   Yes. That is my name. I fear I may have been very rude to you. Allow me to ask your pardon. And will you have the goodness –   (He whispers in her ear.)

MRS. G.   Lord bless us. My dear Mr. Scrooge, are you serious?

SCROOGE   If you please, not a farthing less. A great many back payments are included in it, I do assure you. And this, of course, is your charming daughter. A Merry Christmas to you, my dear.

MISS G.   (curtsies)   Thank you, Mr. Scrooge.

SCROOGE   Delightful child! Now don't forget to come and see me at my office, ma'am.

MRS. G.   I will not forget, Mr. Scrooge.

SCROOGE   Thankee, thankee, and bless you both.

(They go out as BOB and TINY TIM return with FRED.)

BOB   There he is, Mr. Fred, sir, and not himself at all.

FRED   So I see, Bob, he looks very odd.   (To SCROOGE.)
              Uncle!

SCROOGE   Fred, my boy, a Merry Christmas to you, my fine
              fellow.

FRED   (taken aback)   And to you, Uncle.   Are you feeling
              quite yourself?

SCROOGE   Quite myself? Quite myself? And how else would
              I be feeling? But I must confess, Fred, I feel a
              little confused.   I am more happy and elated than I
              have been for many a long year. Is your invitation
              to dinner today still open?

FRED   Still open? You are as welcome as Christmas
              itself.

SCROOGE   Splendid fellow!

              Reprise.   "A Christmas Carol"

ALL   Here's a toast for Christmas Day
                    A toast for Christmas Day
                    Here's to those we love the dearest
                    May they prosper through the year
                    Never shed a tear
                    Be joyful everyone.

CHILDREN   May the people
                    Who are not so bless'd as we
                    Find contentment
                    Each in his own special way
                    Upon this Christmas Day.

ALL   Joyful all the people sing
                    Glory to the new born King.
                    Peace on earth and mercy mild
                    God and sinners reconciled
                    Joyful set the rafters ringing
                    With the Carols that we sing
                    Christmas Carols that we sing.
                    God rest ye merry gentlemen
                    When all is said and done.
                    God bless us everyone
                    God bless everyone
                    Bless us everyone!

              CURTAIN

PRODUCTION NOTE

The staging, moves etc. described in these notes were those used in the original production of the play and are, therefore, known to "work". Obviously many producers will want to stage the show with a completely different approach.

The play is largely episodic and in order to maintain continuity it is essential that each scene should follow immediately on the last, without any pause. This requires careful stage management planning.

In the original production the basic set was black drapes. There was a set of black tabs towards the back, which opened partially in Scenes 8 and 17. There was a set of white tabs one-third upstage, and immediately downstage of these a grey gauze painted in black to represent a pen and ink drawing of a London street scene, following the style of John Leech in the original edition of the book.

Some important pieces of scenery were used more than once and were on trucks for quick changes. These were:

1. Street scene. This consisted of two pieces. One represented the outside of Scrooge and Marley's warehouse, with a window and a practical door. The other side of this same piece was painted as the inside of the same warehouse. The other piece represented the outside of the Poulterer's shop. These two pieces were built in perspective and hinged together at the apex with a removable rod. In the first and last scenes of the play they were set at about 140 degrees, with the apex centre and as far upstage as possible. For the second scene the Poulterer's shop swung parallel to the back of the stage and Scrooge's warehouse trucked round to the position previously taken by the Poulterer's shop, so that the inside then showed.

2. Fireplace. One piece built in perspective represented Scrooge's fireplace on one side (and for this was always set L.), and Cratchit's fireplace on the other side (which was set R.).

3. Window. A practical sash-cord window, used with tattered curtains for Scrooge's room, and doubled for Fred's

parlour with long velvet curtains.

4. Scrooge's Bed. This was a fourposter, again built in perspective so that it looked large without taking up too much space.

All these pieces were made to move easily and silently, since towards the end of the play they were set in view.

Scene I

The scene is set as indicated in the general notes above. The gauze is down. Poulterer is outside his shop talking to the Holly Seller. 1st Lady and Gentleman are near Scrooge's door. 2nd Gentleman is D.C. walking towards R. All are frozen in their positions. The curtain rises as the city clock chimes the hour, and the gauze is lit. The lights on the scene fade up with the strike of three o'clock, and on the last stroke the gauze is taken out. The scene bursts into life as the music starts. There must be much noise and bustle, laughter and cries of "Merry Christmas". 1st Lady and Gentleman walk down L. Holly Seller intercepts them to make a sale. 2nd Gentleman goes out R. Urchin boy runs in R., thumbs his nose at Scrooge's door and collides with the Poulterer, who chases him off L. 2nd Lady and Gentleman enter R., call greetings to 1st Lady and Gentleman. All meet U.R.C. Hot Chestnut Man, Balloon Lady enter as indicated in the score. They and Holly Seller shout each other down for the best pitch and go out. Mrs. and Miss Goodheart enter L., collecting for charity, and go out R. Fred and Topper enter R., buy a bird from the Poulterer, go out L. Centre of stage clears for entry of urchins R. They dance excitedly round and come down for first verse of "Half a Day to Christmas". Holly Seller enters. Adults join in second verse. In third verse Poulterer picks up small girl and kisses her as Holly Seller holds mistletoe over them. During Balloon Lady's song the children follow her round the stage, and then desert her for the Hot Chestnut Man as he sings his song. The two songs can then be sung against each other, half the cast following one, half the other. The Poulterer's song starts at his shop, and after four lines he leads a march of the children, carrying his Norfolk Turkey before him. After this he shoos them off, and only the two Ladies and Gentlemen and the Poulterer are left on for the entry of the three Carol Singers, and then Scrooge. At the end of the scene the cast can swing the scenery round.

Scene 2

Set as indicated in general notes. Cratchit's desk is now L., beneath the window. Scrooge's desk U.R.C. with a hatstand beside it.

Scene 3

White tabs close, and gauze down. The gauze must be slit C. for Scrooge's exit in this scene. Scrooge's door is built on a truck, and is wheeled in from the wings by Marley as the scene changes. Marley is concealed behind the door until his face is lit to show through a gauze inset in the door.

Scene 4

Set as script, with wooden armchair by the fireplace. Much amusing business can be worked into Scrooge getting ready for bed and preparing his supper of gruel while he sings "Fine Man of Business".

Scene 5

In front of white tabs. This is a quick change for Scene 6.

Scene 6

Schoolroom can be simulated by a bookflat painted as panelling with maps, and set R. Small table with tray, glasses and decanter set C. at edge of bookflat. High stool set R. at apex of bookflat. During this scene, Fezziwig's doorway can be set behind the black ready for Scene 8.

Scene 7

White tabs. This is a quick change for Scene 8.

Scene 8

Black tabs drawn partially to reveal doorway to Fezziwig's Office, C. There should be at least one step down from this door so there will be a rostrum behind it with a backing flat or cyclorama. The bookflat used in Scene 6 can be reversed, painted on the other side with an office scene. Fezziwig's desk is on a small rostrum U.R. The other two desks L., one below the other. "Fezziwig's Ball" is basically a Roger de Coverley, and they finish in a semicircle with Mr. and Mrs. Fezziwig in the centre. When the Fezziwig party returns to take part in the song "Gold", it turns into a gay dance. Ebenezer is first whirled round by each of the three girls in turn. The girls then curtsy to their partners and dance in a circle with Ebenezer contained within it. When the verse is taken again softly, the couples make arches. As Ebenezer goes through them he ends R. near to Belle, who is now singing "Heart of Gold" against them. For a moment he makes to go to her, but is pulled back into the dance, and he then abandons himself to it. The song ends after Belle's exit with the party again in a circle round Ebenezer, who has now leapt on a chair.

Scene 9

Set as Scene 4, but fireplace is decorated with greenery.

Scene 10

White tabs and gauze. Snow effect from Effects Lantern.

Scene 11

Fireplace now set R. to show other side. Note that oven must open for the goose to be brought out. Rectangular wooden table. Chair by the fire.

Scene 12

White tabs. Quick change here for Scene 13.

Scene 13

Same table can be used as for Scene 11 to facilitate change, but with an oval top and velvet cloth added to disguise it. Window C. as used for Scrooge's room, but with long velvet curtains drawn. Pedestal with a potted plant could be used to complete the parlour effect, and to give another hiding place for 'Hunt the Thimble'.

Scene 14

White tabs.

Scene 15

Gauze down. Scrooge is down stage of it, Spirit of Christmas Future upstage. Old Joe's shop is set L. This is again a bookflat, built in perspective with a practical door. At this point it is almost closed, showing the outside of the shop, with the apex up C. Half way through the scene it opens to reveal the inside of the shop. This can easily be achieved by means of a long handle projecting through the black tabs. Moving this handle then opens the bookflat.

Scene 16

In front of gauze.

Scene 17

Black tabs partly open to reveal two gravestones on rostrum backed by ornamental iron fence. Backing flat or cyclorama.

Scene 18

Scrooge's bed, window and fireplace are trucked on in view. During this scene the 'graveyard' is struck and the two pieces of street scenery as for Scene 1 are set behind the black tabs ready for the transformation from the bedroom to Scene 19.

Scene 19

If necessary white tabs can be drawn momentarily during Scrooge's "Fine Norfolk Turkey" song, but the change is more effective if it can be done in view.

JAMES WOOD